Mr. Putter & Tabby Run the Race

RUNNING SHOES

CYNTHIA RYLANT

Mr. Putter & Tabby Run the Race

Illustrated by

ARTHUR HOWARD

sandpiper

Houghton Mifflin Harcourt

Boston New York

For Eamon Johnston, who runs a good race
—C. R.

 Published in the United States by Sandpiper, an imprint of Houghton Mifflin Harcourt Publishing Company.
Originally published in hardcover in the United States by Harcourt Children's Books, an imprint of Houghton Mifflin Harcourt Publishing Company, 2008.

SANDPIPER and the SANDPIPER logo are trademarks of Houghton Mifflin Harcourt Publishing Company.

www.hmhco.com

The illustrations in this book were done in pencil,
watercolor, and gouache on 250-gram cotton rag paper.
The display type was set in Minya Nouvelle, Agenda, and Artcraft.
The text type was set in Berkeley Old Style Book.

The Library of Congress has cataloged the hardcover edition as follows:
Rylant, Cynthia.
Mr. Putter & Tabby run the race/Cynthia Rylant;
illustrated by Arthur Howard.
p. cm.
Summary: Mr. Putter is convinced to run in a senior marathon with his neighbor, Mrs. Teaberry, when he learns that second prize is a train set.
[1. Old age—Fiction. 2. Neighbors—Fiction. 3. Cats—Fiction.
4. Running races—Fiction. 5. Physical fitness—Fiction.]
1. Howard, Arthur, ill. II. Title. III. Title: Mr. Putter and Tabby run the race.
IV. Title: Mister Putter & Tabby run the race.
PZ7.R982Mt 2008
[E]—dc22 2007003031
ISBN: 978-0-15-206069-5
ISBN: 978-0-547-24824-0 pb

Manufactured in China
SCP 25 24 23 22 21 20 19 18 17 16 15
4500816097

PUTTER
+
GAZETTE

1

Find Your Sneakers

It was April.
Mr. Putter and his fine cat, Tabby,
were full of April energy.
They always got extra energy in April.
Flowers were blooming,
birds were singing,
showers were showering. April!
Mr. Putter and Tabby felt it.

Mrs. Teaberry next door must have felt it, too.
She called Mr. Putter one April morning.
"There's a race," she said.
"A race?" asked Mr. Putter.
"A marathon!" said Mrs. Teaberry.

Uh-oh, thought Mr. Putter.

He was sure Mrs. Teaberry was going to ask him to run the race with her.

"Will you run the race with me?" asked Mrs. Teaberry.

Mr. Putter gave Tabby more cream.

"Aren't we too old to run a race?" asked Mr. Putter.

"It's a *senior* marathon," said Mrs. Teaberry.
"Nothing but old people!"
Mr. Putter gave Tabby another biscuit.
"I have not run anywhere in thirty years,"
said Mr. Putter.
"I don't think I remember
how to run."

"There are prizes," said Mrs. Teaberry.
"Prizes?" asked Mr. Putter.
Mr. Putter *loved* prizes.
"One is a train set," said Mrs. Teaberry.
"Really?" asked Mr. Putter.
"With lights and switches and tunnels,"
said Mrs. Teaberry.
"Really?" asked Mr. Putter again.

"The train set is second prize,"
Mrs. Teaberry said.
Mr. Putter could not imagine a
train set being *second* prize.
It should be first.
"What is first prize?" asked Mr. Putter.
"Golf clubs," said Mrs. Teaberry.

Mr. Putter did not play golf.
He had tried once, but he and Tabby
kept getting lost.
Mr. Putter did not want golf clubs.
"I want that train set," said Mr. Putter.
"I knew you would," said Mrs. Teaberry.
"Find your sneakers."

2

Toes and Tea

Mr. Putter started training for the marathon.
It was not easy.
It took him four days just to find his sneakers.
Then he had to work out.
Mr. Putter did not want to work out.
He wanted to eat muffins with Tabby.

But he knew that Mrs. Teaberry
was working out because
sometimes her good dog, Zeke,
ran by with a jump rope in his mouth.
(When Zeke wanted to play,
he took things and *ran*.)
So Mr. Putter had to work out, too.

He decided he would touch his toes
thirty times every day to make up for
the thirty years he'd forgotten to run.
The first time Mr. Putter tried to touch his toes,
he could not reach them.
He touched his knees
instead.

He touched his knees twice, and then he had
a cup of tea with Tabby.
The next time Mr. Putter tried to touch his toes,
he tried ten times, and he never got there.
But he enjoyed his tea with Tabby very much,
and he decided knees were just fine.

Zeke kept running by with his jump rope,
Mr. Putter kept touching his knees,
and Tabby had lots of tea.

Things were going great.

The
Zekers

3

Seniors!

It was finally the day of the senior marathon.
Mrs. Teaberry and Zeke were very excited.
Mrs. Teaberry had made special outfits for both of them.
Zeke still had a jump rope in his mouth.
(Zeke had become very attached to his jump rope.)

They all drove to the race.
When they arrived,
they saw many seniors lining up to run.
Zeke and Tabby got settled on top of the car.

Mr. Putter and Mrs. Teaberry got settled near the starting line.

"I didn't know there were this many old people," said Mr. Putter.

"Oh, we're everywhere!" said Mrs. Teaberry.

Mr. Putter looked around.

He saw a lot of old people touching their toes.

Uh-oh, thought Mr. Putter.

Everyone got in line.

“I hope you win that train set,”

said Mrs. Teaberry.

“I hope you come in first,” said Mr. Putter.

The horn sounded.

And the seniors started running!

5
23
16

4

The Race

Everybody passed Mr. Putter.
Everybody except two people.
Two people who tripped and fell and never got up.
But everybody *else* passed Mr. Putter.

Mrs. Teaberry was way out in front.

Mr. Putter was way behind.

Tabby was asleep.

And Zeke had a jump rope in his mouth and wanted to play.

That's when the race took a turn.

Suddenly there was confusion.

A dog with a jump rope was running the race!

All of the seniors tried to pass him.

They started bumping into one another.

Some of them got bumped right off the road.
Some of them stopped running
and started arguing.
More of them tripped.

But one of them wanted a train set so badly
that he ran right past everybody,
and grabbed hold of that jump rope,
and held on for dear life.
Zeke finally had someone to play with!
Zeke was so happy he ran even faster.
This made *Mr. Putter* run even faster.

Mr. Putter did not let go.

He wanted that train set.

He passed one runner after another

after another after another.

Then he passed Mrs. Teaberry.

And then . . .

HE WON THE RACE!!!

Everyone cheered! Everyone clapped!
Everyone was happy!

Everyone, that is, except Mr. Putter.

He had just won a set of golf clubs that had no lights and no switches and no tunnels.

Phooey! thought Mr. Putter.

5

Perfect Prizes

But things worked out after all.

Because who came in second? Mrs. Teaberry!

So she and Mr. Putter swapped prizes.

Mrs. Teaberry took her golf clubs home.

And Mr. Putter took home the best train set he had ever seen in his life.

And for the rest of April, Mrs. Teaberry
and Zeke came back from the golf course
and went straight to Mr. Putter's house
to watch his trains.

Mr. Putter had a train hat.

Mrs. Teaberry had a golf hat.

Zeke had a jump rope.

Tabby had a nap.

EAT

And things worked out perfectly.

BARBER